EVERY-DAY DRESS-UP

by Selina Alko

Alfred A. Knopf

New York

I used to only play princess
until Mommy showed me pictures
and told me stories of real, great women.

Now dressing up is an adventure
when, every day of the week,
I am a daring new dame!

On **Monday**, I put on goggles.
With cardboard wings, I'm ready to go.

I'm Amelia, First Lady of Flight!
Like a bird, I soar smoothly in the sky.

On **Tuesday**, I slip into a dazzling dress. Standing up onstage to scat . . .

I'm Ella, Queen of Jazz!
I sing my heart out to a full house of fans.

On **Wednesday**, flag waving, I march and I fight, so every woman will have the right to vote.

I'm Elizabeth, Super Suffragist!
I proudly pave the way for First Lady Eleanor
and Supreme Court Justice Sonia.

On **Thursday**, I button up my lab coat, using test tubes and beakers and trial and error.

I'm Marie, Star-Studded Scientist!
I make medicine to cure the sick.

On **Friday**, I tie on an apron and stand tall,
teaching fancy French cooking to Americans.

I'm Julia, Chef Extraordinaire!
Fish in hand, I declare, "Bon appétit!"

On **Saturday**, I don shiny slippers and a terrific pink tutu. Center stage, I turn, jump, and plié.

I'm Maria, Prima Ballerina!
Spinning like a diamond,
I twinkle and sparkle for the crowd.

On SUNDaY, I draw
a thick black brow.
Sock monkey perched in pose . . .

I'm Frida, Prized Painter!
Like Alice and Georgia, I add color to canvas,
creating forests and flowers and pictures of me.

After trying on gowns of greatness,
I fold up the props and put them away.

I love to sing, dance, draw and paint,
cook, take trips, help people, and lead the way.

And when I'm older, I hope
to have my own outstanding outfit,
so that little girls will sport costumes of me!

BIOGRAPHIES OF A FEW GREAT WOMEN

Amelia Earhart (1897–1937)
Aviator Amelia Earhart was the first woman to fly solo across the Atlantic Ocean! She wrote books about flying and was a great inspiration to many women. She tragically disappeared while flying over the central Pacific Ocean in 1937.

Ella Fitzgerald (1917–1996)
The American jazz and scat-singing vocalist Ella Fitzgerald sang her way through her rough childhood. She began performing at the Apollo Theater in Harlem and eventually recorded more than two hundred albums. Her music is much loved by people all over the world.

Elizabeth Cady Stanton (1815–1902)
A leading figure of the early American women's movement, Elizabeth Cady Stanton was a social activist and abolitionist before narrowing her focus to suffrage (the right of women to vote and to run for office).

Eleanor Roosevelt (1884–1962)
First Lady of the United States from 1933 to 1945, Eleanor Roosevelt was an advocate for civil and human rights. She was a delegate to the United Nations and became an internationally known author and speaker, nicknamed the "First Lady of the World."

Sonia Sotomayor (1954–)
Sonia Sotomayor's Puerto Rican roots make her the first Hispanic justice on the U.S. Supreme Court. She was born in the Bronx, New York, and in 2009 became the 111th justice and only the third woman in the Supreme Court's history.

Marie Curie (1867–1934)

Scientist Marie Curie was honored with not one but two Nobel Prizes, in physics and chemistry! Polish-born, she became a French citizen and directed some of the world's earliest studies of cancer.

Julia Child (1912–2004)

The American chef, author, and television personality Julia Child introduced French cuisine to the American public. Her first book, *Mastering the Art of French Cooking,* led her to star in many popular television programs in which she taught cooking.

Maria Tallchief (1925–)

Of Osage Indian and Scots-Irish ancestry, Maria Tallchief was America's first prima ballerina! Her family's Native American ceremonial dances sparked Maria's early interest in dancing. Ballet captured her heart, and she eventually became the prima ballerina of the New York City Ballet.

Frida Kahlo (1907–1954)

The Mexican painter Frida Kahlo is best known for her intensely personal self-portraits. She used vivid, vibrant colors—perhaps reflecting her lifelong struggle with pain due to a traffic accident when she was a teenager.

Georgia O'Keeffe (1887–1986)

Georgia O'Keeffe was one of the most important artists of the twentieth century. Born on a farm in the American Midwest, she later moved to New Mexico, where she made large-scale paintings of flowers, rocks, shells, animal bones, and landscapes.

Alice Neel (1900–1984)

The American portrait painter Alice Neel spent some time in Cuba, where she developed her lifelong political consciousness and commitment to equality. She lived most of her life in New York, where she painted her family, politicians, locals, and strangers.

To Ginger & Greta,
and girls everywhere

THIS IS A BORZOI BOOK PUBLISHED BY ALFRED A. KNOPF

Copyright © 2011 by Selina Alko • All rights reserved.
Published in the United States by Alfred A. Knopf, an imprint of
Random House Children's Books, a division of Random House, Inc.,
New York. • Knopf, Borzoi Books, and the colophon are registered
trademarks of Random House, Inc. • Visit us on the Web!
www.randomhouse.com/kids • Educators and librarians, for a variety of
teaching tools, visit us at www.randomhouse.com/teachers
Library of Congress Cataloging-in-Publication Data
Alko, Selina. • Every-day dress-up / Selina Alko. — 1st ed.
p. cm. • Summary: A young girl imagines her own future as she puts on
costumes and pretends to be great women from history, including Amelia
Earhart and Eleanor Roosevelt. • ISBN 978-0-375-86092-8 (trade) —
ISBN 978-0-375-96092-5 (lib. bdg.) — ISBN 978-0-375-98460-0 (ebook) •
[1. Costume—Fiction. 2. Imagination—Fiction. 3. Biography—Fiction.
4. History—Fiction.] I. Title.
PZ7.A39843Eve 2011   [E]—dc22   2010001604

The illustrations in this book were created using gouache and collage.

MANUFACTURED IN CHINA
October 2011
10 9 8 7 6 5 4 3 2 1
First Edition

Books That Inspire

ELIZABETH LEADS THE WAY:
ELIZABETH CADY STANTON AND THE RIGHT TO VOTE
by Tanya Lee Stone; illustrated by Rebecca Gibbon

FRIDA
by Jonah Winter; illustrated by Ana Juan

HOW WE ARE SMART
by W. Nikola-Lisa; illustrated by Sean Qualls

MASTERING THE ART OF FRENCH COOKING
by Julia Child, Louisette Bertholle, and Simone Beck;
illustrated by Sidonie Coryn

SKIT-SCAT RAGGEDY CAT: ELLA FITZGERALD
by Roxane Orgill; illustrated by Sean Qualls